The Girl Who Danced with Giants

WRITTEN BY
Shawna Thomson

ILLUSTRATED BY
Tamara Campeau

For Miss Ali Kadlun,
who always loved to play
Jon's harmonica as loud
as she could.

Table of Contents

Chapter 1

That's So Boring

Iviit and Pauloosie were supposed to be helping their family at their summer camp. Instead, they had run away together to play hide-and-seek with Iviit's dog, Qaniq.

"I see you, Pauloosie!" yelled Iviit, pouncing on her brother's back.

"Bah!" groaned Pauloosie, shaking off his sister. Qaniq ran up to his two favourite humans, barking and licking Pauloosie's face. "All right. You hide, I'll count. One... two...three..."

"PAULOOSIE!" came a loud bellow. The children's *ataattiaq* and *amaamak* were standing on a bluff overlooking the area where they were playing. "All of the men are waiting for you! Get up here now," said their ataattiaq.

Iviit tried to make herself low to the ground to avoid being seen as her brother started trudging up the hill toward his ataattiaq. "And you, Iviit!" her amaamak snapped, sounding annoyed. "We have skins to clean."

Iviit groaned and followed her brother. "Why do I always have to clean the skins?" she grumbled as she caught up with her brother. "I want to go hunting with you."

"You're a girl," explained Pauloosie. "I have to grow up and be a good hunter to provide for my wife. And you have to grow up to be a wife and make clothes for your hunter husband."

"That's so boring," Iviit complained. Pauloosie shrugged and followed their ataattiaq. At least he was nice enough to wave sympathetically at her as he followed the eager hunters out on the land.

Iviit had to spend the rest of the day sitting in the hot sun with her amaamak, *anaanak,* and aunties cleaning skins until her arms ached and her ulu was dull. She was so grumpy she even looked enviously at Qaniq, who stayed close by, either gnawing on an old bone or chasing *hikhiit.*

The only good thing about the day was that she got to listen to some of her anaanak's stories of times from long ago. Anaanak spoke of the little people who would sometimes help a lost traveller find his way home. And she told of terrible giants who could eat a whole caribou herd until, stuffed and lazy, they might fall asleep for a thousand years or more.

That night, the men came home with three caribou they had caught on their hunt. The whole summer camp stayed up under the midnight sun to celebrate. Pauloosie had caught his first caribou of the summer. He knew it was hard for Iviit to hear about all of his adventures when she had been stuck at home, so he convinced Ataattiaq to let Iviit play his special harmonica.

The harmonica was bright red and made the most glorious noises when blown into. Ataattiaq had traded many fox furs for it with the men at the Hudson's Bay Company trading post. It was one of his most prized possessions, and he only let Iviit play with it on special occasions.

To say thank you, Iviit wanted to show her family the new song she had made up. She liked it best of all the songs, because it let her make a lot of noise and dance as loudly and happily as she could.

> *"This is my dancing song,*
> *It helps me dance so loud,*
> *I play my dancing song,*
> *And I go POUND POUND POUND!!"*

On the last notes, Iviit jumped up and down and shouted as loudly as she could. She looked around, expecting her family to be impressed. Instead, her amaamak shook her head and said, "Oh, Iviit. Why can't you be nice and quiet like your girl cousins? Go to bed and stop making so much noise!"

Iviit was very sad.

Chapter 2

Let's Get Out of Here

The next day, Iviit woke up to the sound of her amaamak calling her. "Iviit! Hurry up. More skins to clean! The men have already gone hunting. Get out of bed, you layabout!"

Iviit was so mad she could have cried at the thought of another day cleaning skins. Her arms still hurt. She thought about pretending to be sick, but she didn't want to stay in the tent all day. As she was thinking of what she could do, she noticed her ataattiaq's beautiful red harmonica hanging up in its place. Right away, she knew what she would do. "I'll be right there, Amaamak!" she called, carefully unhooking the harmonica and sliding it into the pocket of her dress. "I'm just going to feed Qaniq first."

"Well, hurry up!" called Amaamak.

Trying not to think about what would happen when she got home, Iviit slipped out of the tent and found Qaniq lying in the shade. "Come on, boy," she whispered to Qaniq. "Let's get out of here."

The girl and her dog went running off as fast as their legs could carry them. They ran for a long time. Iviit wanted to get far enough away that her amaamak wouldn't want to come and look for her. That way she and Qaniq would have all day to play. Finally, they collapsed in the shade of a big hill by a little pond. Iviit spent some time watching the clouds roll across the clear blue Arctic sky, pointing out all the shapes she saw to Qaniq.

He didn't seem interested, though, and Iviit soon got bored of this. She sat up and looked around. For the first time, she noticed the strange shape of the hill in front of them. It looked exactly like a large man lying down with his head resting on his arms, fast asleep. "Look at that hill, Qaniq," Iviit said. "I bet we could see everything from up there!"

She and her dog raced up the hill, scrambling over big rocks and pulling themselves up as fast as they could. Qaniq was quite a bit faster than Iviit and got to the top first, barking at his human to hurry up.

Once she reached the top and had time to catch her breath, Iviit took a look around. The whole tundra stretched out before her. She could see the little brown dots of her family's summer camp over to the west. If she squinted, she thought she could pick out which tiny figure was her amaamak. And that little figure looked mad.

Trying not to think about that, Iviit pulled out her ataattiaq's harmonica. "Would you like to hear my song, Qaniq?"

He barked twice, which Iviit took to be dog-speak for "Yes, please!"

"This is my dancing song,
It helps me dance so loud,
I play my dancing song,
And I go POUND POUND POUND!!"

Iviit played as loudly and as long as she could! She blew into the harmonica with all the power in her lungs. And she stomped her feet with all the power in her little legs. The whole time, Qaniq barked and ran around her, looking like he was trying to join in the singing and dancing.

Suddenly, the whole earth gave a great heave. Iviit and Qaniq were pitched forward, and Iviit almost lost hold of the harmonica. The earth started to shake...and twist...and groan?

Iviit and Qaniq scrambled to try to keep their feet steady, but the ground they had been dancing on was quickly becoming vertical. Iviit felt herself falling through the air, her feet above her head and Qaniq's tail in her face.

She landed with an "oof" on something soft, and then started to rise again.

She opened her eyes, then closed them, then opened them again, unable to understand what she was looking at.

Chapter 3

Hey, You!

Iviit was lying in the palm of a man so large the only word she could use to describe him was "giant." He had lifted her up so that his eyes, each the size of a stretched sealskin, could look at her closely. His mouth was a gaping hole full of ferocious teeth. Looking down, Iviit could see all the lichen and Arctic grass that had grown over him were falling to the ground far below as he shook himself awake.

She heard whimpering and saw that Qaniq was trapped in the giant's other closed hand. Her poor dog was yelping and squirming, trying to free himself from the giant's meaty paws. The giant looked away from Iviit and licked his red lips in anticipation as he eyed Qaniq.

"Yummy snack," he chortled to himself in a deep voice that seemed to reverberate in Iviit's bones.

Iviit watched in horror as the giant lifted Qaniq to his open mouth, ready to devour her dog.

Knowing she had to act quickly, Iviit started jumping up and down on the giant's hand. She jumped harder than she had ever jumped in her dancing song. "HEY, YOU!" she yelled, louder than she had ever yelled in her whole life. Which, for a girl who makes as much noise as Iviit, is really quite loud.

Surprised by her sudden fury, the giant froze and turned his attention back to Iviit. "You can talk?" he asked in surprise.

Having that big face and voice trained on her, Iviit swallowed thickly to stop her

voice from shaking. "Of course I can talk! And you had better leave my dog alone!"

"But I am so hungry," groaned the giant, looking rather upset. "I feel like I haven't eaten in a thousand years."

"Well, that's your own fault for sleeping so long!" Iviit retorted, sounding braver than she felt. "You slept so long lichen grew on your nose!"

The giant crossed his eyes to look at his nose and saw that Iviit was right. He reluctantly put the little girl and her dog down on the ground so he could scratch his nose. Iviit thought about trying to make a run for it, but she knew that with his massive legs, the giant would easily catch her no matter how fast she ran.

Once his nose was de-lichened, the giant started eyeing Qaniq again.

"Don't even think about it!" Iviit said in her most threatening voice. She stood in front of Qaniq, glaring heatedly at the giant.

The giant seemed to consider her for a second, and then he sat down with a big huff. His weight smashing into the earth made the ground shake so much that Iviit was sure they must have felt it back at the summer camp. "But I'm soooo hungry."

Iviit relaxed a bit, thinking the giant might not have a lot of fight in him. "Well, I'm sorry about that," she said, trying to sound sympathetic. "But you can't eat Qaniq. He is my best friend in the whole wide world."

"I miss my best friend," the giant moaned. "I haven't seen him in so long."

The giant looked so miserable sitting on the ground, rubbing his belly, that Iviit found herself feeling sorry for the creature. "Where does your friend live?" she asked.

"He lives..." The giant paused and looked around. "It's near...well...I don't quite seem to remember." This thought made him look even sadder, and Iviit knew she couldn't leave him sitting by the lake looking so unhappy.

"I think we got off on the wrong foot," she said, trying to sound friendly and

moving closer to the giant. "My name is Iviit. What's yours?"

"My friends call me Kaaktuq," the giant said. Iviit tried not to laugh, but the name was very fitting. It meant "hungry" in Inuinnaqtun.

"Well, I can be your friend," she suggested, hauling herself up on his giant foot to stand a bit closer. "And if you let me and Qaniq go, we can come back tonight and bring you some food."

Kaaktuq looked quite cheered up by that thought. "You promise?"

"Oh, yes," Iviit said confidently. "I'll see you tonight...with lots of food."

Chapter 4

A Giant Problem

Iviit was in a lot of trouble when she got back to camp. Her amaamak yelled a lot. And then her anaanak and ataattiaq talked a lot. And then she and Qaniq were both sent to their tent with no supper. Since she was planning on sneaking out in a few hours when everyone else was asleep, she didn't mind this very much.

She was even happier when Pauloosie popped into her tent with his pockets full of bannock and *piffi*. "That was a silly thing you did today," Pauloosie said. "They'll never let you do what you want if you won't do what you're told."

"I know, I know," Iviit said, not really paying attention to her brother's words as she tucked the food into her loon bag. "Can you get more of this? Like a lot more?"

As soon as Iviit knew the rest of the people at the camp were asleep, she and Qaniq snuck out and went back to the place where she had met Kaaktuq.

"You came back!" Kaaktuq clapped his hands in delight as Iviit started to unpack her loon bag. She handed him chunks of fresh bannock and strips of piffi. He shovelled them all into his mouth and looked around for more when he was finished. Even though it was late in the night, the sun was still high in the sky, so Iviit helped Kaaktuq look for ptarmigan eggs to eat.

When Kaaktuq was finally full, Iviit and Qaniq taught him Iviit's dancing song. She hadn't dared to bring the harmonica out to the pond again in case she got caught, but with Kaaktuq's booming voice and large stomping feet, she almost didn't notice it was missing.

"This is my dancing song,
It helps me dance so loud,
I play my dancing song,
And I go POUND POUND POUND!!"

Just before morning, Iviit ran back to camp and slipped into her tent before anyone noticed she was missing. Before she knew it, her amaamak was waking her up to start her chores. She was very tired, but she didn't want to draw any attention to herself, so she sat quietly and picked away at her caribou skins. As she scraped, she listened to the ladies talking.

"Naujaq said he felt the earth moving yesterday," one of her aunties told the group. "He had gotten up in the middle of the night and the whole tent was shaking."

"What would make that happen?" asked Iviit's amaamak.

Anaanak looked worried. "My amaamak used to tell me that when the ground shakes, it means there is a giant nearby."

Iviit felt her cheeks go red as her anaanak continued. "But there hasn't been a giant in these parts for years and years."

Iviit let out a sigh of relief as the other ladies moved on to a new topic. She and Kaaktuq would have to be more careful.

Iviit and Kaaktuq had a wonderful summer together. They played games and searched for eggs. They danced and sang songs. Later in the summer, they picked berries, and Iviit showed Kaaktuq where the biggest berries grew. As the season started to change, Iviit worried about what to do with Kaaktuq when the winter snows came and it was time to move away. It would also be harder to find food for him when the storms drove away a lot of the animals her family feasted on in the summer and fall.

Her problems grew bigger shortly after the first big snowfall at their camp. She overheard some of her uncles talking together. "They were massive footprints," said her uncle Naujaq. "Bigger than any bear I've ever seen. And shaped like a man's foot!"

"There is a giant around here

somewhere," her uncle Qaqqaq told the other men. "We must find it and kill it before we leave for the winter camp, or it will follow us."

Iviit snuck away immediately to go and warn Kaaktuq. He was sitting by the edge of the lake, looking at the thin layer of ice that was beginning to creep around the shore. He didn't hear her coming, and when Iviit got closer, she realized the giant was crying big, hot giant tears that melted the snow when they fell on the ground.

"What's the matter?" she asked him, alarmed.

Kaaktuq wiped his eyes and gave her a shaky smile. "I'm okay, Iviit," he said. "I am just missing my family. This time of year we normally go together to our winter camp and enjoy seal hunting and playing games in our *igluit*."

Iviit offered to dance the dancing song with Kaaktuq to cheer him up, but he didn't want to. She was beginning to realize she had a giant problem on her hands.

Chapter 5

Humans Don't Come Here

Iviit knew she had to help Kaaktuq get back to his family. Not just because he was sad, but for his own safety. But neither she nor Kaaktuq had any idea where the Giant Winter Camp might be. There was only one person Iviit knew who had knowledge about giants. So that night, when the rest of her family was starting to head to their tents to sleep, Iviit went to her anaanak and told her everything.

Her anaanak listened to everything Iviit had to say with a serious look on her face. "Giants are dangerous, my dear," she warned her granddaughter. "How do you know he isn't taking you to the Giant Winter Camp so that he and his family can eat you?"

"He wouldn't do that!" Iviit said. "He's my friend."

Anaanak made a *harrumph* noise in the back of her throat. "Then I guess you had better take me to meet this giant."

The next day, Iviit took her anaanak to meet Kaaktuq. Kaaktuq was nervous at first, but after a few minutes of talking, they both warmed up to each other. Anaanak agreed that Kaaktuq seemed like a relatively friendly giant and not particularly likely to eat Iviit or any of her family members.

"Can you help him find his way to the Giant Winter Camp?" Iviit asked nervously as Kaaktuq and Anaanak shared some tea and bannock. Anaanak had brought her biggest mug for tea, but it still looked like a thimble in between two of Kaaktuq's fingers.

"Oh, yes," Anaanak said. "That won't be a problem. We'll leave when the rest of the family leaves for our own winter camp. It will be a long journey, though. Is that dog of yours ready for a long sled run?"

Iviit assured her anaanak that he was. "But what about Ataattiaq and Amaamak?" she asked. "Won't they mind us going off by ourselves? We can't tell them about Kaaktuq!"

"You just leave them to me," Anaanak said, with a mischievous twinkle in her eyes.

Iviit never knew how her anaanak did it, but when the rest of the family left with the sleds for winter camp, she and her anaanak had their own sled, pulled by Qaniq and two other dogs from her ataattiaq. They waved goodbye to the rest of the family and went to pick up Kaaktuq.

Iviit, Kaaktuq, and Anaanak travelled together for many days and weeks. Qaniq and his dog friends were tireless, always up and ready to go each morning for another day of racing across the frozen land. Iviit sometimes ran alongside the dog team, untangling their leads and directing them forward. Other times, she sat curled up in the sled, nestled in furs, listening to her

anaanak call out commands to the dogs and the heavy thump of Kaaktuq's footsteps following along beside them.

Iviit lost track of how many days they travelled. It was winter now, and the days were shorter. Soon they had to keep travelling long into the dark night. Finally, just when it seemed like the journey would never end, they saw it in the distance: the Giant Winter Camp. It was hard to miss, a whole village of absolutely massive igluit that towered over the hills surrounding them. Iviit could see a few giants, some even bigger than Kaaktuq, sitting outside the igluit.

"How have I never heard of this place?" Iviit asked her anaanak.

"Humans don't come here," Anaanak said, her mouth set in a firm line. "I hope these giants remember Kaaktuq."

Iviit felt a flutter deep in her stomach as she looked at Kaaktuq. She noticed he looked about as nervous as she felt. "I hope so, too," Kaaktuq agreed in his big booming voice.

Chapter 6

One Last Time

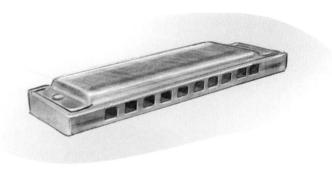

Qaniq pulled the sled closer to the giants and their igluit. He seemed a little unsure as well, stopping every few steps to sniff the air. There were two giants watching them approach, munching quietly on muskox leg bones. When they were about 50 paces from the giants, Qaniq and the other dogs started whining and lay down, refusing to go any farther. Iviit swallowed and pushed back her blankets, getting ready to say hello to the giants. She really hoped they weren't hungry.

"KAAKTUQ!" came a great booming voice. Another giant came bounding up from inside the Giant Winter Camp. As he ran, the whole ground shook, and Iviit sat back down quickly so she didn't fall out of the sled.

"AIVIQ!" bellowed Kaaktuq, running toward his friend. They gave each other a giant hug, jumping up and down in joy and making boulders of snow fall from the surrounding hills and smash down among the igluit.

More giants came out to see what all the fuss was about. They all seemed very happy to see Kaaktuq and started hugging him and giving him pats on the back. Iviit's friend was finally home.

"Time to say goodbye, Iviit," Anaanak whispered in her ear. "The Giant Winter Camp is no place for a human."

Iviit knew her anaanak was right. She fought back tears as she said goodbye to Kaaktuq. He lifted her up and gave her one last hug. He wiped away tears as he put her back on the ground. "I won't forget how you helped me," he said. "Thank you, Iviit."

"Just remember, if you get sad, you can always play the dancing song," Iviit reminded him. She thought it might be a good reminder for herself, too.

"Why don't you have your dance one last time?" Anaanak suggested, surprising Iviit by pulling the red harmonica out of the pocket of her parka.

This brought a grin to Kaaktuq and Iviit's faces. Iviit raised the harmonica to her lips and started to play.

> *"This is my dancing song,*
> *It helps me dance so loud,*
> *I play my dancing song,*
> *And I go POUND POUND POUND!!"*

All the giants and Qaniq and even Anaanak joined in. They all made as much noise and pounded their feet as loudly as they could. It was the loudest song that was ever played in the history of the Arctic, which, as the giants will tell us, is a very long time indeed.

Chapter 7

Aren't You Coming?

A few weeks later, Iviit, Qaniq, and Anaanak arrived at their family's winter camp. Pauloosie came running out of their amaamak's iglu and gave Iviit a big hug, telling her how much he had missed her and asking all kinds of questions. Iviit wasn't sure how to answer her brother, but Anaanak intervened. "It was women's work, Pauloosie. You men don't need to worry yourselves about it!" Pauloosie knew better than to ask any questions after that.

The next day, Iviit was still feeling a little sad. She was happy that Kaaktuq was back with his family, but she missed her friend. It didn't help when Pauloosie went running out of the iglu, excited to head out wolf hunting with the men. "I'll bring you back a big wolf fur for your parka," he promised, disappearing out the door.

Iviit gave a big sigh and buried her head in Qaniq's fur. She darted back up when she heard slow footsteps come in through the door. Her ataattiaq was standing in the entrance to the iglu, looking at her expectantly.

"Aren't you coming, Iviit?" he asked, holding a spear out to her.

Iviit was speechless, staring at the beautifully made weapon in front of her. "Me? Really?" she asked.

Her ataattiaq nodded with a smile. "If my granddaughter is brave enough to dance with giants, surely she is brave enough to come hunting wolves."

Iviit stared up at her ataattiaq. "She told you?"

"I didn't like it," her ataattiaq answered. "But I don't have the courage to tell your anaanak 'no' when she has her mind set on something. I think you two have that in common. Now, get your things, child."

Iviit let out a cheer and started to grab all of her winter clothing. Her ataattiaq tossed her a warm hunting parka. He turned to leave, and then paused. "Just one thing, Iviit..."

"Anything!" she cried happily.

"The harmonica stays at home."

Inuinnaqtun Glossary

Notes on Inuinnaqtun pronunciation: There are some sounds in Inuinnaqtun that may be unfamiliar to English speakers. The pronunciations below convey those sounds in the following ways:

- A double vowel (for example, *aa*, *ee*) creates a long vowel sound.
- Capitalized letters indicate the emphasis.
- **q** is a "uvular" sound, which is a sound that comes from the very back of the throat (the uvula). This is different from the **k** sound, which is the same as the typical English **k** sound.

Aiviq AI-viq	**name, meaning "walrus"**
amaamak a-MAA-muk	**mother**
anaanak a-NAA-nuk	**grandmother**
ataattiaq a-TAA-ti-aq	**grandfather**
hikhiit HIK-heet	**ground squirrels**
iglu IG-loo	**snow house**
igluit IG-loo-it	**snow houses**

Iviit I-veet	**name, meaning "grass"**
Kaaktuq KAAK-tooq	**name, meaning "hungry"**
Naujaq NOW-yaq	**name, meaning "seagull"**
Pauloosie POW-loo-see	**name**
piffi PIF-fi	**dried fish**
Qaniq QA-niq	**name**
Qaqqaq QAQ-qaq	**name**